Big Dog and Little Dog
Making a Mistake

Dav Pilkey

Houghton Mifflin Harcourt
Boston New York

Library of Congress Cataloging-in-Publication Data is on file.
ISBN: 978-0-544-65114-2 paper over board
ISBN: 978-0-544-65122-7 paperback

Manufactured in China
SCP 10 9 8 7 6 5 4 3 2 1
4500575152

Ages	Grades	Guided Reading Level	Reading Recovery Level	Lexile® Level
4–7	K	D	5–6	50L

For Samantha Jeanne Wills

Big Dog is going for a walk.

Little Dog is going, too.

Big Dog and Little Dog
see something.

What do they see?

Big Dog thinks it is a kitty.

Little Dog thinks so, too.

Ssssssssssss.

But it does not *smell* like a kitty.

Big Dog smells bad.

Little Dog smells bad, too.

Big Dog and Little Dog

had a bad day.

They are going home now . . .

. . . just in time for a party!

❧ Story Sequencing ❧

The story of Big Dog and Little Dog's mistake got scrambled! Can you put the scenes in the right order?

A

B

C

D

E

answer key: E, A, C, D, B

❀ On the Run! ❀

Is that a kitty? Use your finger to trace
the best path through the maze for
Big Dog and Little Dog to reach it.

❧ Word Scramble ❧

These words from the story got mixed up! Can you unscramble them and point to the correct words in the word box? Try writing a new story with these words!

Word Box

ESE	PARTY
TYPRA	SMELL
MEHO	BAD
DAB	WALK
LELMS	KITTY
KALW	HOME
TYKIT	SEE

Bow-Wow!

Check out these amazing dog facts.

- A German shepherd named Orient guided the first blind man to hike the entire Appalachian Trail— 2,100 miles!

- Norwegian lundehunds have six toes on each paw so they can climb steep cliffs and their ears fold down and seal shut to keep out dirt.

- Dogs and people have many of the same organs, but dogs do not have appendixes.

- Almost all dogs have pink tongues except for the chow chow and the shar-pei. Their tongues are black!

- Dalmatian puppies' fur is completely white when they are born and their spots appear later.

❀ Fill-in-the-Blank ❀

Use the pictures to choose the missing word from the word box!

Word Box

smell
home
kitty
bad
walk
party

Big Dog and Little Dog are going

for a _____ .

Big Dog and Little Dog think they see a _____ .

The kitty does not _____ like a kitty.

Big Dog and Little Dog smell _____.

Big Dog and Little Dog go _____.

They are just in time for the _____!